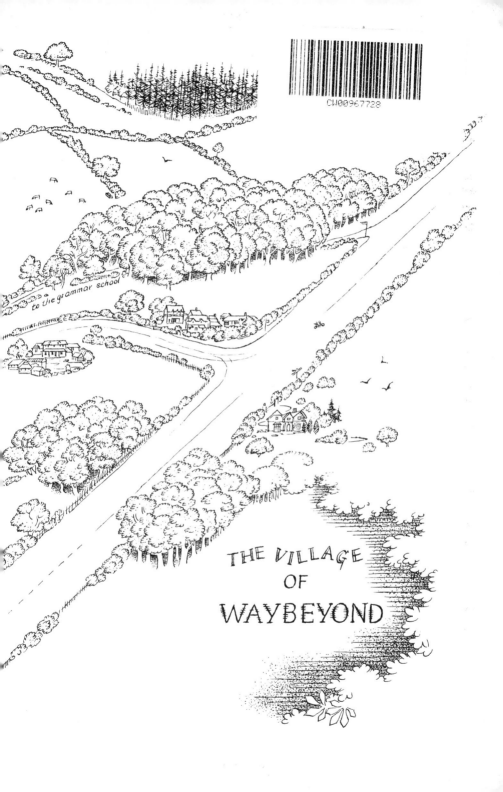

to the grammar school

THE VILLAGE
OF
WAYBEYOND

Tales of Waybeyond

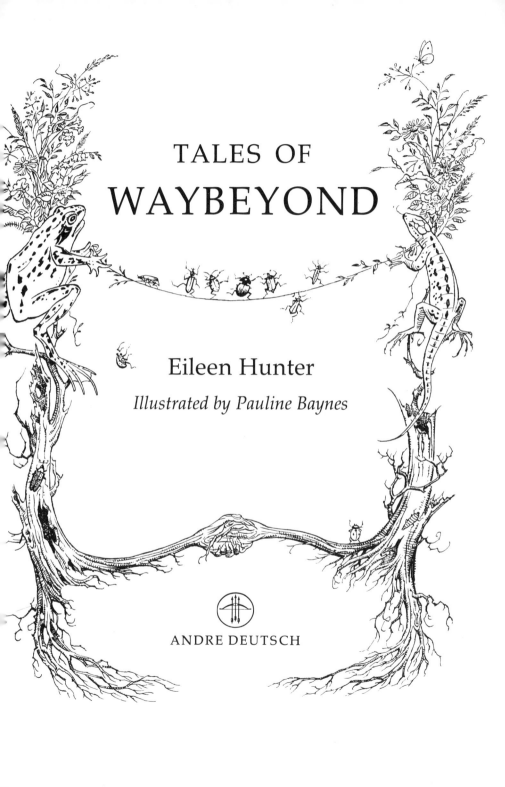

TALES OF
WAYBEYOND

Eileen Hunter

Illustrated by Pauline Baynes

ANDRE DEUTSCH

First published 1979 by
André Deutsch Limited
105 Great Russell Street London WC1

Text copyright © 1979 by Eileen Hunter
Illustrations copyright © 1979 by Pauline Baynes
All rights reserved

Set, printed and bound in Great Britain by
Cox and Wyman Ltd, London, Fakenham and Reading

British Library cataloguing in Publication Data

Hunter, Eileen
    Tales of waybeyond.
    I. Title
    821'.9'14   PZ8.3

    ISBN 0-233-97084-3

First published in the United States of America 1979

Library of Congress Number
79-64184

To Narisa with love

Contents

A Cat and Mouse Story

Two spinster cats in an ivy-clad house,
Kept as a pet, a pretty white mouse.
They were both vegetarians, and so the mouse knew
He'd never be grilled or made into a stew.
Miss Elfrida, the elder, was Tabby and trim,
Miss Polly was rounder, grey-striped, not so slim,
While as for their pet, fed on eggs, cream and milk,
He was charmingly plump and his fur was like silk.
He wore a pink ribbon, was brushed every day,
And slept in a basket of sweet-smelling hay.

Waybeyond was their village, well shaded by trees,
Where the folk were all kindly and go-as-you-please.
Where the houses were neat and beautifully kept,
With gardens flower-filled and paths always swept,
And a nice little store that sold everything
From butter and flour to postcards and string.
The place was in fact, so peaceful and pretty
That all were content – no one pined for the city.

But one bright summer's day, as the two spinster cats

Took tea on their lawn, wearing large shady hats
Tastefully trimmed with ribbons and posies,
And Mousie was dozing among the red roses,
An opulent car slid up to their door,
And out stepped a cat they had not seen before.
Tall, ginger and handsome, impeccably dressed,
Elfrida and Polly were greatly impressed;
What could he be doing in quiet Waybeyond,
Far from the town where he clearly belonged?

'I fear I intrude, forgive me, I pray,
But could you direct me, I've quite lost my way?'
The ladies both bowed, they were very well-bred,
'We'll gladly assist you,' Miss Elfrida said,
'But first, won't you join us, the tea's freshly made,
And Miss Polly will place you a chair in the shade?'
At the end of an hour of agreeable chat,
They learned their new friend was an aristo*cat*,
Sir Montague Tawney, a bachelor, who
Wrote books on good food and gave fine dinners too.

Just as they reached this point in their talk,
Mousie awoke and frisked out for a walk.
Sir Montague stared, his eyes bulged from their sockets,
His claws were extended – concealed in his pockets,
He managed to say, 'What a dear little fellow,
Now if you'll excuse me, I think I must go.'
For he knew if he stayed, he would cause an upset
By making a pounce at their unusual pet.
So they told him the way and waved him goodbye;
But all the way home, he dreamed of Mouse Pie,
Of Mouse à la mode or egg-breadcrumbed and toasted,
Of creamy Mouse Mousse and mouse baked or roasted.

When curtains were drawn and lamps brightly glowing,
The ladies sat down to their knitting and sewing,
Miss Polly purred praises of Sir Montague,
'*So* charming – *so* courteous and good-looking too!'
Miss Elfrida, more thoughtful, said, 'I can't forget
The strange parting look he cast at our pet.'
Miss Polly, indignant, cried, 'How can you think
Anyone of his station could possibly sink
To regarding a creature so pretty and sweet
As our little Mousie as something to eat!'
Miss Elfrida smiled grimly, 'I hope I'm not right,
All the same we should not let our pet out of sight.'

But Mousie was young and Mousie was sprightly,
And much supervision both daily and nightly,
Made him rebellious and long for a run
Down to the village and out in the sun,
While the ladies, poor dears, grew so anxious and worn
That one afternoon after tea on the lawn,
They both nodded off and took forty winks,
Enabling their pet to get up to high jinks.

But because he had noticed their great agitation,
He'd sized-up the perils of his situation.
Though seeming carefree as he scampered about,
He was on the alert and kept a look-out;
And well that he did, for he suddenly saw
On the latch of the gate, a large ginger paw.
And in crouched Sir Montague, sly as you please,
Tempting the mouse with a fine piece of cheese,
While hidden from sight behind his broad back,
He clutched in his paw a sinister sack.

Mousie pretended to sniff with delight
The aroma of cheddar, then, as he was bright,
Knew surprise was important, so sprang in the air
And instead of the cheese, bit Sir Montague's ear.
Oh what a commotion and what an uproar,
Such as quiet Waybeyond had not heard before.
*Cat*erwauling with pain, Sir Montague tried
To shake off the mouse, who his efforts defied.
He held fast with his teeth and needle-sharp claws,
Rocking with glee at Sir Montague's roars.

Elfrida and Polly woke up in a fright,
And went into action to put matters right.
They both seized the sack and, opening it wide,
Called, 'Jump, Mousie, jump!' – he was soon safe inside.
Miss Elfrida said, 'Sir, we shall not entertain
You or your kind here ever again.
Though titled and rich, you're greedy and sly.
There is the gate, sir, we wish you goodbye!'

Bleeding, disgraced, with head hanging down,
Wicked Sir Montague went back to town.
Though, in spite of himself, he admired the brave mouse,
Who, when calm was restored to the ivy-clad house,
Had for his supper Sir Montague's cheese,
Served up on toast with some fresh garden peas.
And when curtains were drawn and lamps brightly glowing
And the ladies sat down to their knitting and sewing,
They both sighed with pleasure as they looked around.
All was in order; and there, safe and sound,
Mousie slept in his basket. How thankful they felt,
And content with their home where such happiness dwelt.

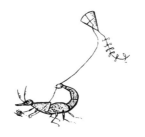

Sir Samuel Mole

The manor house at Waybeyond – Mole Hill,
Has always had an awesome reputation.
For old Sir Samuel Mole, who lives there still,
Is known for fits of rage and irritation;
He has some cause, it's true, being almost blind,
And all alone but for a single soul,
An ancient butler, last of a large crew
Who served him once, but, in the end, declined
To stand the tantrums of the titled mole,
And their mean pay, for he was stingy, too.

No one has been inside the house for years,
But tales abound of winding corridors,
Down which Sir Samuel feebly gropes and peers,
Tapping his cane along the dusty floors
Of gaping chambers where the velvet sheds
From furniture, lop-leggèd with neglect.
A sly wind mutters at the broken panes,
Where rustling silken curtains hang in shreds.

17

The agile spider spins a web unchecked,
And the rotted roof lets in the winter rains.

Through extra strong binoculars each day,
Though no one ever came in his direction,
Sir Samuel passed a few blank hours away,
Submitting the empty landscape to inspection.
Yet one March morning, specially aggrieved,
Because he always so disliked the spring,
Trudging along the road towards his gate,
Badger, the portly postman, he perceived.
Post for him! A most unheard of thing;
He worked himself at once into a state.

'Tom,' he bawled, 'There's someone at the door,
Stir yourself, and answer it, you oaf.
I don't know what I keep a butler for,
When all you do is drowse around and loaf!'
Slowly old Tom, who also had bad sight,
Drew back the rusty bolts and clanking chain,
And in the musty hall, the door yawned wide.
There, blinking in the unaccustomed light,
Threat'ning the cowering butler with his cane,
Stood old Sir Samuel, now revealed inside.

Badger was surprised, he'd always found
Folk were glad to hear his cheerful knock,
And often smiled to greet him on his round,
So such ill-temper came as quite a shock;
He decided therefore not to wait about,
Sure no cup of tea would come his way,
(The house gave him the creeps in any case).
So from his bag, he took the letter out,

Gave it to the Mole and said good-day,
And gladly left the glum and gloomy place.

Staring at the letter with suspicion,
Sir Samuel turned it upside-and-then-down,
Mumbling he'd a dreadful premonition
It was from Cousin May who lived in town.
And he was right, for so it proved to be;
For when he'd summoned Tom to hear the news,
And brought himself at length to break the seal,
He turned quite pale with rage, so Tom could see
The letter was no pleasure to peruse;
And at the end, he gave a piercing squeal:

'Coming to stay! Ah, what an awful thought;
How can we put her off? We have no phone;
Here tomorrow – notice is so short!'
He sank back trembling, with a hollow groan.
'We'll manage, sir,' said Tom. 'Now, never fear –
How nice to see that sweet Miss May once more.
What's brought her to these parts, if I may ask?'
'No, you may not,' his master snapped. 'Look here,
Such sentimental chatter I deplore;
To get this house to rights will be *your* task!

The last time she was here was long ago,
When we had staff – and though I loathed them all,
The place was well-maintained and kept just-so;
She thought it very charming, I recall.'
Old Tom looked round and sighed, what would she say
(A lady of the old school as she was,
Used to a certain comfort, quiet refined)
To the ravaged rooms, eroded by decay,

The rutted drive all overgrown with moss,
And bindweed round the ruined roses twined.

What he must do, the well-trained servant thought,
Was to soothe his master – that poor gentleman.
Completely useless. He had not been taught,
To sweep or clean or even use a dustpan.
'You've had a trying morning, sir,' he said,
'So don't you think it would be for the best,
To go up to your room, lie down at ease,
And when you're settled comfortably in bed,
I'll come and fetch your best suit to be pressed,
And bring you a hot posset, if you please?'

Only too willing to oblige, his master
Went upstairs, and soon his hearty snores
Informed old Tom he now could get on faster,
And free from interruption, with the chores.
It would be wise, he thought, if they made use
Of the huge kitchen as a living-room,
And, hoping Sir Samuel would not cause dismay,
Or shock his guest with vollies of abuse,
On all the other rooms' neglected gloom,
He locked the doors, and hid the keys away.

By dawn, the kitchen shone and sparkled brightly,
And Miss May's little room was fairly clean.
But poor old Tom – the years did not sit lightly –
Was tired and weary as he'd seldom been.
He brought a would-be dainty breakfast tray,
And shook the Mole from sleep by half-past-eight,
Laid out his best black velvet suit, and then
Binoculars – to look out for Miss May.

And, though inclined to fret and agitate,
The Mole was spying out the land by ten.

From far away, he saw her car draw near,
And soon, he stood to greet her in the hall.
Like all who haven't met for many a year,
Each falsely cried, 'You haven't changed at all!'
Miss May was diplomatic, quiet, well-dressed,
And felt regret and even consternation,
At her impulsive visit to a place
Where she remembered being much impressed
By style and comfort – not dilapidation.
Concealing her feelings with an easy grace,

She asked to see her room; unpacked, descended,
Ate odd food in the kitchen without fuss,
And having decided – 'least said, soonest mended,'
Ignored the shut-off rooms, did not discuss
Or ask to see the mouldering, mossy grounds,
But did her petit-point and made small talk.
Though when her cousin's eyes began to close,
She tip-toed off and swiftly made the rounds,
Of shuttered rooms and sad neglected walks,
And returned before he woke up from his doze.

When next day dawned, Miss May was up betime,
And helped by Tom with scrubbing-brush and pail,
Made some impression on the layers of grime.
But by lunchtime, felt both tired and frail;
Even so, she cooked delicious food,
That Mole ate up, and praised up to the skies.
He did not lose his temper once all day.
So after dinner, still in mellow mood,

She tackled him, asked if she might advise –
He should get much more help without delay.

This did not please Sir Samuel at all,
For glad to have some help when it was *free*,
He *enjoyed* being mean, and really saw no call
To make improvements he could hardly see.
He croaked in answer that he thanked her, and
Would with care consider her kind thought,
But now was tired and must retire to rest –
He shuffled off, his manner so off-hand,
That Tom knew well, her scheme would come to naught,
And begged her not to mind or be distressed.

Eventually, Miss May stayed on a week,
Feeling it was her duty to help Tom,
But thought her cousin had enormous cheek,
For while they toiled, he idled with aplomb,
Relished with greed the tasty food he ate,
Indulged in long siestas or a stroll,
Carped about money spent on soap and vim,

And was in fact, so inconsiderate,
Miss May had need of all her self-control,
Not to reveal just what she thought of him.

So when the moment came to say goodbye,
Car at the door and all her cases packed,
She attempted even at the last to try
To persuade him to accept the obvious fact –
Without more help and careful management
His house and garden – everything he owned
Would soon return to chaos and decay.
She realised he was glad that when she went,
Action of any kind could be postponed,
And he could waste and dream his life away,

Secure from the busy world, where featureless,
The slow days pass and nothing much occurs;
Where clocks have stopped, and time seems motionless,
Sir Samuel is contented, for that's what he prefers!

Success Story

In Waybeyond, the general store
Was owned by an old sea-dog,
Once afloat now based ashore,
His name was Captain Mogg.

He'd many a yarn about his trips
When skipper of a trawler,
And tales to tell of old tall ships,
Though tall – his tales were taller!

Captain Mogg had grizzled hair,
And though not young was limber.
His trim little shop with a nautical air,
Was built of old ships timber.

On a sign that hung above the door,
He'd printed 'Second to none',
And this was not surprising for
His store was the *only* one.

A bakery there was, it's true,
Where bread was baked at night,
And sold from a basket, crisp and new,
By a spaniel, brown and white.

The spaniel's sister baked the bread,
And slept from dawn till dark,
'It's a dog's life, mine,' she sometimes said
With a melancholy bark.

Once a month, a traveller came,
And Mogg replenished his stocks,
But, bored one day with seeing the same
Pots and pans and crocks,

'I'm tired of these,' he snapped, quite cross,
And got an offended look,
As the traveller giving his head a toss,
Closed his order-book.

'If you want to see some slap-up things,
First-class stuff – brand-new,
I've novelty lines in frillies and rings
That a lady could sell – but not you!'

'No matter,' said Mogg, 'I'd like to see
All you've got in those cases,'
And swept aside the grocery
To look at trinkets and laces.

Prettily glittering, cobweb-fine,
Mogg quite lost his head,
Bought up all the traveller's line,
And forgot that he had said:

To sell such dainty frills and gew-gaws,
A female would be required,
Not an old sea-dog with clumsy paws,
Late R.N. retired.

Recalling his words, Mogg worried indeed,
But doggedly set his jaw;
Pressed on with plans at maximum speed
To extend the scope of his store.

And as in that free and happy place,
Permission was not needed,
Construction work went on apace,
And Captain Mogg succeeded

Within a month in building on
An elegant boutique,
Where polished woods and brasses shone,
And the goods were quite unique.

But catching sight of himself in one
Of the counters fronted in glass,
He saw he'd look a figure of fun
And custom would be sparse

Unless he found, as the traveller said,
A lady who was efficient.
Sales would not 'steam full ahead',
And profits would not be sufficient.

So now when the local ladies went
To shop at their village store,
They remarked that Mogg was different,
For he'd never stared before.

Now he looked them up and looked them down,
In a manner most ill-bred,
That made the ladies flounce and frown,
And order by phone instead.

Feeling utterly scuttled one day,
And certain that he'd been daft,
He suddenly spied across the way,
What he termed 'a trim little craft'.

Basket on arm and apron neat,
Brisk and alert her eye,
She tripped along the village street,
Not bold – yet not too shy.

Mogg seized his trusty telescope,
And got her well in view.
How despair would change to hope,
If she'd sign on as crew!

Out of his shop, he sprang with a bound;
Alas, she'd vanished from sight!
But there upon the path he found
Her silken scarf, snow-white.

It lay outside the bakery door,
So he boldly rang the bell,
And when she appeared, he shook her paw,
And gave her the scarf as well.

'It's strange we haven't met,' he said,
'Not at all,' said she,
'For during the day, I am in bed,
As I bake at night, you see.'

But as my brother's gone to bring
His bride from Faraway,
I've baked *and* been delivering,
Just for once today.

When they're wed, it's their desire
To run the bakery,
While I've decided to retire,
Which very well suits me.'

'But won't the days seem long,' said Mogg,
'With nothing much to do;
When I've the most delightful job
That's just the thing for you?'

He took her to his smart boutique,
And, dazzled by what she saw,
Agreed to work a trial week,
But in the end stayed four.

She pleased him so with her pretty ways,
And excellent business brain,
He'd nothing to blame and much to praise,
And begged her to remain.

She sometimes cooked nice meals for Mogg,
When their work was over,
And he thought himself a lucky dog,
With all four paws in clover.

And although he'd been a sailor bold,
It was hard for him to find
Words that truly would unfold
What he had in mind.

Till going through his stock one day,
He chanced on a plain gold ring,
He chose it as the simplest way
Of explaining everything.

So the ring was given – a bride was won,
And in time above the door,
Was proudly printed 'Mogg and Son,
The *Department* Store'.

And when the traveller comes round,
He's asked to lunch or tea,
For as Mogg remarks, 'Through him I found,
A partner, wife and family.'

The Prodigal Badger

Badger, the postman, and his sturdy wife,
Were both well-liked and very much respected
And took an active part in village life –
Yet had a son whose ways were unexpected.
For, to his parents sorrow and regret,
He did not follow in their worthy pawmarks,
But when still young got into the wrong Set,
Idled around, went in for foolish larks,
Left home; was heard of next in Faraway,
And after that there was no news for years,
Except that he'd acquired a 'soubriquet',
'Artful Badger' – adding to their fears,
Which all were realised. O pain and grief,
They heard that he'd become a common thief.

In Waybeyond, for long there'd been a joke,
That when the letters were delivered late,
It meant, so said the knowing village folk,
Badger had lingered by each door or gate
Because he'd news or scandal to impart.
But now he hurried by with head bent low,
His sack no heavier than his aching heart,
Hoping the whole village did not know.

But every now and then, a nod, or look,
Confirmed his fears – the news had got around:
He knew his son was known to be a crook.
He hastened home, his eyes upon the ground,
For, what was worse and made him doubly sad,
His boy was doing well by being bad.

Once he had dreamed that Bevis – his son's name,
Starting as clerk might one day be postmaster,
Not well paid jobs, nor leading to the fame
Which he had gained dishonourably much faster!...
Meanwhile in Faraway, his erring son
Just 'worked' at night; gambled with crooks all day,
(They cheated – as did he – so neither won),
At poker in a down-at-paw café.
These were the friends who'd taught him how to rob,
And cheat the law, from whom he'd learnt too well –
So now he was the leader of their mob,
As he was smart and eager to excel.
Qualities that surely should have lit
Pride in his father's heart – not broken it!

One Autumn, funds and spirits both being low,
Mobster-Mouse arranged with Cracksman-Cat,
(A show of paws agreeing yes or no,)
With Badger, Pincher-Pig and Hare Bad-hat,
That they should team-up in a country job.
Although they knew the Badger was not fond
Of 'working' out of town they planned to rob
A local post-office – at *Waybeyond*.
Cat, a master of the double-cross,
Observed that Badger paled, and this reaction,
As Cat was rival for the post of boss,

Gave him extreme, but hidden satisfaction,
And when he got the gang to vote his way,
He had no doubt the Badger was at bay.

Bevis stepped forward, holding up a paw,
'I hope I've led you well,' he quietly said,
'Safely on the wrong side of the law,
And abided by your vote, but now instead,
Be clear, I won't have anything to do
With robbing Waybeyond, and you may find
I'm on the other side. I'm warning you.
So why not drop this plan and change your mind?'
Pig looked dubious, so did Hare Bad-hat,
To cut this caper on their own seemed mad,
But weakly, they supported Mouse and Cat,
While Bevis found he secretly was glad,
That, once resolved his hometown to defend,
He felt his life of crime was near its end.

That night, he slipped away and by the dawn,
Entered the shady woods he knew so well,
Around the tranquil place where he was born;
And chose a hiding-place, just parallel
With where the small post-office stood. And so,
Well camouflaged, he lay till almost dark,
While village folk he knew went to-and-fro,
Including his father and the postal-clerk.
And when the doors were locked and shutters closed,
He ventured out and with a skeleton-key,
Broke-in, as easily as he'd supposed.
And inside in the gloom could faintly see,
All was unchanged; the same as, when a boy,
To sort the mail, had been his pride and joy.

Resolved to give the gang a nasty shock,
He hid behind some mail-bags on the floor.
And when he heard a key turn in the lock,
He bounded forward and flung wide the door.
Crowded on the step, the startled gang
Were so surprised, they tumbled down inside –
Where Bevis, paws up at the ready, sprang
And laid about them. They were stupified.
And soon found out how bravely badgers fight
Defending what they feel to be their own;
So that ere long their one idea was flight.
At first he punched and hammered them alone,
Till, woken by the din, to the gang's dismay,
Some villagers turned out to join the fray

Including Bevis' father, and how glad,
He was to recognise his doughty son,
Fighting on the same side as his dad,
And winning though the odds were four to one!
But Bevis had his plans, and as he hit
Cat on the jaw, he muttered in his ear,
'Swing-door at back, now cut and run for it!'
Through two black eyes, Cat looked his thanks sincere,
Sprang to the back and tipped the wink all round,
While Bevis obliged by knocking Pig – not out –
But through the door and onto open ground.
And then with relish gave the Hare a clout,
While his father – no fool – understood,
Pretended to chase the robbers through the wood.

And so the gang all made a get-away,
Grudgingly grateful to their one-time chief,
Who, having been their friend, did not betray

Them, nor let them really come to grief. . . .
Meanwhile, at Waybeyond, a new day dawned,
And all were keen to shake our hero's paw,
Till tired out and craving sleep, he yawned.
At which his father firmly said, 'No more!'
And took him home to where his mother waited.
Tactful and kind, she merely hugged him tight,
And by her silence, clearly demonstrated
True affection, let him sleep till night.
And when he woke, he found the table laid
With dishes he liked best which she had made.

So Bevis Badger, once more took his place,
Beside his happy parents and did well,
A credit and no longer a disgrace.
And though, no doubt, he might again rebel,
If life held no excitement, no surprises,
He likes his job as driver for the parcel-post –
It's more adventurous, he recognises,
Than office work. Yet what delights him most,
Is every aspect of security.
In Waybeyond and villages around
He has become the great authority,
And if asked why his knowledge is so sound
On all devices to frustrate a break-in,
He quietly smiles – a reminiscent grin. . . .

As for the gang, they nevermore were seen,
For he had warned them, let them go scot-free,
And though they were not straight, they were not mean,
Which proves untrue what everyone believes:
As sometimes there *is* honour among thieves!

Millicent Mouse

At the end of the village, a neat little house,
In a neat little garden, about half-an-acre,
Displayed a neat sign reading 'Millicent Mouse,
Ladies Outfitter, Exclusive Dressmaker'.

In the thick laurel hedge, birds nested unseen,
And mingled their song with the sound from indoors,
The rackety-clack of a sewing-machine,
That rattled away with scarcely a pause,

Except when Miss Millicent fitted the dresses,
Coats, blouses and skirts she made with such care;
Few of them failures, mostly successes,
That all were agreed stood years of hard wear.

Not swinging or with-it, perhaps one might say,
Not up-to-the-minute or trendy or smart,
But with fasteners and buttons sewn on to stay,
And strongly stitched seams that did not come apart.

One day, great excitement, Miss Millicent heard
That her niece, Marigold, was going to wed,
Not a mouse-of-the-village as she'd have preferred,
But a pop-singer mouse from Remoteness instead.

Her niece had arranged that the next afternoon,
She would call on her aunt to discuss and decide
On clothes for the wedding (a month hence in June),
For bridesmaid and page – and, of course, for the bride!

Miss Millicent's parlour was soon upside-down,
As she looked out her patterns of satin and lace,
Tulle for a veil and pearls for a crown,
And fashion-plates scattered all over the place.

For being romantic, she always had found,
Thoughts of a wedding made her so elated,
Her heart beat too fast, her head whirled around,
And she got in a muddle – a thing that she hated.

All the same, the next day, the table was laid,
With all her best china, and by half-past-four
A selection of buns and cheesecake she'd made,
When a huge motor-bike spluttered up to her door.

In helmet and goggles and jeans carefully frayed,
There was her niece getting down from the pillion,
Wearing a jacket of bright yellow suede,
Covered with badges in green and vermillion.

Beside her, Mick Pop-Mouse, in black leather dressed,
Stood languidly by as she shook out the dust,
A wealth of gold chains displayed on his chest,
Playing it cool and not getting fussed.

It was Millicent later, who felt fussed, for she
Could not get to know him as he hardly spoke,
Except to remark that he never drank tea,
Did not like cake and much preferred Coke.

While she and her niece talked of satin and lace,
She felt that his silence was most disapproving,
And at the word 'veil', she saw him grimace,
And soon he said, 'Luv, we ought to be moving.'

Miss Millicent saw Marigold was distressed,
That he wanted to go with nothing decided,
But being polite, she thought it was best
To pretend all was well though she thought him misguided.

But when they were gone, she saw clearly now,
He thought her a frump and scorned her ideas,
But she made a great effort and managed somehow
Not to give way or burst into tears.

She found she was right, for soon Marigold wrote,
To say she had talked with her bridegroom-to-be,
Who felt that their wedding should strike the right note,
And be modern in style and as trendy as he:

So they'd already bought, when shopping one day,
A ready-made dress of cheesecloth with smocking,
Trimmed with wide bands of cotton crochet,
Cheesecloth! – Miss Millicent thought it was shocking,

Its place was the kitchen – it had many uses;
She used it herself, her stockpot to clear,
For making cream-cheeses and straining fruit juices,
Really, the tastes of the young were most *queer*!

Miss Millicent sighed – ah well, never mind,
She wished them both well and there had to be change,
She had plenty of work and must be resigned
That to Mick, it was *she* whose notions were strange...

By the time she received her engraved invitation,
The wedding was due in less than a week.
Then her niece rang her up – oh what a sensation,
So choked up with tears, she scarcely could speak.

It appeared her new dress had come home from the shop,
And while trying it on, she had caught a loose thread
That unravelled the smocking and couldn't be stopped,
The whole dress was ruined, poor Marigold said.

On the following Monday, her wedding was due,
The shops were all closed as it was the weekend,
So out of the question to find something new,
Could Millicent help her, and be a real friend?

Without hesitation, her brisk little aunt,
Said, 'Bring me the dress and we'll put it all right.'
For she had been taught 'Can is better than can't',
And was more than prepared to sit up all night.

And when Marigold had shown her the frock,
And then put it on, it was perfectly plain,
The machinery used to stitch and to smock,
Had slipped on the yoke, which must be done again.

Miss Millicent frowned, the best thing she thought
Was to cut out and smock a new bodice completely.
But where to find stuff when time was so short,
To make a good job and finish it neatly?

The style was quite pretty, she had to admit,
The cheesecloth draped well and did not hang badly,
The sleeves, finely tucked, were a very nice fit,
But without some more stuff – she shook her head sadly.

At her expression, poor Marigold's eyes,
Again filled with tears; but before they could fall,
Her aunt dashed to the kitchen – and, marvellous surprise,
Cried, 'Here is some *cheesecloth* – now this solves it all!'

'There'll just be enough, this piece is brand-new,
Leave the dress here, and run home, dear child,
You'll have it tomorrow with smocking done, too,'
For the first time that day, poor Marigold smiled.

Having waved her goodbye, Miss Millicent started
Cutting and tacking and stitching and basting,
Working better alone when her niece had departed,
Too well aware, she'd no time to be wasting.

She was greatly relieved when her task was completed,
And the smocking was finished and carefully pressed,
For she felt she could say without being conceited,
That smocking was one of the things she did best.

She ran to the phone and told Pop-Mouse to come,
He thought it was 'smashing' that she'd been so quick,
'Think of Marigold's face when I bring the gear home,
You're top of the bill, you're aces, my chick!'

Though not understanding too well what he meant,
Miss Millicent felt as he twice shook her paw,
That she'd made a new friend, and as she was content
To have helped the young people, she asked nothing more.

The wedding-day dawned, it was sunny and fair,
And Miss Millicent, wearing her best powder-blue,
Eager to see what the young guests would wear,
Was early at church and got a front pew.

She was glad that she had for she was astounded
At the remarkable outfits that all the girls wore;
Picture-hats, mob-caps, berets, abounded,
With breeches and boots or skirts sweeping the floor.

As for the boys, each was a dandy,
Strutting in denim or sharply-cut suits,
In T-shirts, frogged jackets or shirts striped like
                                         candy,
In cowboy or Russian or cavalier boots.

But how startled she was when the bridegroom
                                         arrayed
In a *white satin* suit and shirt ruffled with lace,
And a fanciful waistcoat of silver brocade,
Entered the church and went to his place.

The *bridegroom* in *satin, cheesecloth* for the bride,
By conventional standards, it really was wrong,
How topsy-turvy, Miss Millicent sighed,
Yet her disapproval did not last for long;

For there in the church, filled with brightly-clad mice,
Excited and happy, *she* felt light-of-heart,
They were handsome and cheerful and friendly
                                         and nice,
And did not make her feel she was old and apart.

And the moment her niece advanced down the aisle,
Looking graceful and sweet with a pretty bouquet,
In a wreath of fresh flowers, with a tremulous smile,
Miss Millicent's doubts had all melted away.

And at the reception, all glasses were raised
In a toast to 'the lady who saved the bride's gear'.
Miss Millicent blushed – pleased to be praised.
And touched by their words as they sounded sincere.

After the bride and the groom had departed,
Miss Millicent, left in her parlour alone,
In spite of herself, felt rather down-hearted;
Though she wouldn't have done so if she had known

That more than one guest who'd admired the bride's dress,
And noted the smocking and finish by hand,
Had asked Marigold for her auntie's address.
She found herself, soon, very much in demand.

For her beautiful handwork became all the rage,
Trendy and Ethnic and with-it, therefore
Two smart young assistants she had to engage,
As she'd so much more work than ever before.

Pleased though she was at the turn things had taken,
With the folk of the village, she made a great point,
Of making quite sure they did not feel forsaken,
Or that their noses were put out of joint.

For she knew them so well; not only their tastes,
Their friendships and feuds, their family history,
But even the size of their hips and their waists –
To the village dressmaker, few things are a mystery!

In fact, she was often the first one to hear
Of an engagement, a wedding, a happy event,
As thinking immediately, 'What shall we wear?'
They all hastened round to consult Millicent.

But because of her un-common-sense and her tact,
Which came from the heart, as she loved Waybeyond,
The charm and the peace that their restless world lacked,
Was felt by the young, and they became fond

Of not only the handwork she did with such skill,
But the place where she lived and her many good friends.
It was no passing craze – they are going there still,
At least they still were, when this chronicle ends!

Pig-Headed Peregrine

Peregrine, the Porker's only child,
Encouraged by his parents fond embrace,
Set out for school with trotters neatly filed,
Bristles trimmed and rosy well-scrubbed face,
With a satchel holding books and pencil-case.
By working hard a scholarship he'd won,
And at the Grammar school secured a place.
Though poor, his parents proud of what he'd done,
Had bought a brand-new outfit for their clever son.

Pleased with his well-pressed suit and collar clean,
He turned to wave as he went down the lane,
Determined to do well, be brisk and keen,
And excellent reports and marks obtain.
But, alas, these hopes and good resolves were vain,
For from behind a leafy chestnut tree,
A bulldog bully, no one could restrain,
Plus two cronies, so they numbered three,
Fell on the startled pig with barks and yelps of glee.

But crafty as well as cruel, they took great care
Not to overdo their mean attack,
Knowing their teacher who was stern and fair,
And knew their ways, might well give them the sack,
If another pupil turned up blue and black.
So they smeared his collar, scuffed his shoes,
And tore his cuffs, and trousers at the back.
Much dishevelled but without a bruise,
He came in, flustered, late for class without excuse.

The master was affronted when he saw
This slovenly addition to the school,
Slow in the uptake, late and what is more,
So nervous that he seemed an utter fool.
At break, he was held up to ridicule,
With cries of 'Dirty pig' and 'Where's your sty?'
But somehow he contrived to look quite cool,
And being determined not to cringe or cry,
Managed to stop a tear from springing to his eye.

The first week passed and every single day,
The wretched gang of bullies lay in wait,
Smudged his homework, threw his books away,
Then ran ahead to watch him come in late,
And grinned to hear the teacher fulminate;
But the sturdy little pig throughout it all,
Did not sneak, did not retaliate,
But dodged and ducked, took many a nasty fall,
And judged that though the dogs were big, their brains were
                                                        small.

Imagine how his parents were upset,
To see him coming home in such a mess,

In fact his mother very often wept,
As she mended, darned and ironed, and in distress,
Begged 'Tell your teacher', but without success.
For Peregrine had quite made up his mind,
And refused to change it even under stress,
As he'd a plan and hoped the dogs would find
Only one pig, too much for three of them combined.

When Peregrine was home at the weekend,
One afternoon, he knocked upon the door,
Of an uncle, who was also his good friend,
Known better as 'Unbeaten Battling Boar',
Who lived alone and was a bachelor.
'Come in,' the veteran cried, 'and take a pew,
What've you come to see your nunky for,
How's eddication, what's it done for you,
You don't look bright and chipper like you used to do?'

Peregrine told all and said how much
He'd like to learn the art of self-defence
From the Battling Boar himself for such
Expert help would give him confidence.
His uncle nodded, pleased with his good sense,
Then lit his pipe and puffed it, deep in thought,
Keeping his little nephew in suspense,
While he considered if he really ought
To distract an intellectual lad from work to sport.

At length, he spoke, 'Now mark well what I say,
The Noble Art's not only brawn but brain,
Till end of term, you go another way
To school and each weekend come here and train.
All right, they'll think you're scared, but that's a gain,

For when they're off their guard, you'll close right in,
With each move carefully planned in your campaign,
Feint left – lead right and land one on the chin,
Aim always for a knock-out, that's the way to win!'

So Peregrine, who knew the country well,
Every morning took a different route,
And the dogs although they mounted sentinel,
And often yapping chased in hot pursuit,
Found him not such fun to persecute.
His work improved, the boxing made him fit,
Yet to pay the gang out, he was resolute,
And Battling Boar was happy to admit
His nephew, being pig-headed, wasn't one to quit.

He made such progress during his vacation,
His uncle was quite pleased with Peregrine,
Joked he'd be 'a fisticuff sensation,
A lasting credit to an old has-been;'
But added gravely, 'you must have a scheme
To divide the leader from the other two,
For to take on three to one you would be green.

Get him alone whatever else you do,
And as you are so brainy, I'll leave that to you!'

First day of term, the little pig set out,
Earlier in the morning than before.
His parents, worried that the bulldog lout
Would persecute their blameless son once more,
Tried to look cheerful as he left their door,
But Peregrine went bravely on his way,
Hoping for peace although prepared for war,
Flexed his muscles, ready for the fray,
Tried dancing footwork in the style of Cassius Clay.

And when the chestnut tree came into view,
Where the gang of bullies always lay in wait,
Two tins of dogmeat (and an opener too),
Out of his satchel, he produced as bait.
And well thought-out to vex and aggravate,
He threw both tins, half-opened on the ground,
So that the meat was hard to extricate,
Besides the rough-edged tin might well be found
To pain cause and discomfort to a greedy hound.

This done, he got behind the tree and hid,
Till saunt'ring, arm-in-arm, the bullies came,
Paused to sniff, then slavering, all did
As he'd designed, for three of them made claim
On but two tins of meat, and to their shame
Rowed and growled and snarled in horrid greed,
Until their leader furious became
Because his jowls and jaws began to bleed.
He limped away and left his friends alone to feed.

From behind the tree, a small pink whirlwind spun,
Attacking him with science and precision,
Rat-tatting like a tiny Gatling gun,
And startled by this unexpected vision,
The bulldog in a state of indecision,
Was toppled by a swift punch to his head.
While, still intent upon the meat's division,
Indifferent to his prostrate form outspread,
His greedy, so-called friends went guzzling on instead.

It was Peregrine, in fact, who brushed his coat,
And helped him to his paws, for he'd been taught
By uncle that a winner should not gloat,
And not forget to shake hands when he'd fought,
And accept defeat or victory like a sport.
Astonished at this novel attitude,
By now the bulldog, rather overwrought,
Instead of snarling, being rough and rude,
Was quiet and thoughtful, one might almost say subdued.

His boon companions, finished with the feast,
Hang-dog looked, as well indeed they might,
Having not helped him in the very least,
Pretended that they thought *he'd* won the fight,
But found this nonsense was dismissed outright.
'It's time for school,' the bulldog boomed, 'Let's go,
Or are you going to hang around till night?
I'm a bit groggy still, so I'll go slow,
And follow with my friend, the champion boxing pro!'

Later, somewhat battered, arm-in-arm,
They both walked in and took their usual places,
The teacher who was tactful, remained calm,

But among the pupils there were snide grimaces,
And sniggers at the bulldog's battle-traces.
While Peregrine at break was most surprised,
To find the fight had acted like a charm,
For until now, he had not realised,
How many friends he had, who now materialised!

Battling Boar was mighty proud to hear,
The fearful bully had been clean knocked-out.
'Best piece of news I've heard this blinking year,
After this there'll never be no doubt,
Who'll come off best in a *professional* bout.'
Next day, the teacher – a surprise approach –
Called Peregrine and asked him to find out
Whether he thought the subject he could broach,
And ask his uncle if he would be boxing-coach.

As it so happened, Battling Boar was glad,
For being retired, he often found life slow,
And thinking of past glories made him sad,
So he agreed and told the teacher so,
And both insisted bullying must go.
And go it did, for when the school was taught
Skilful exchange of blow and counter-blow,
By well-matched equals in fair contest fought,
To knock the weak about, no longer seemed good sport.

So all was well, the Battler, much respected
Coached all the bulldogs to be heavyweights,
Peregrine worked hard and as expected,
Went to college and did well in Greats.
But always kept in training, for he thought although
His talents were scholastic – still you never know!

A Take-Over Bid

The inn at Waybeyond, the *Friendly Paw*,
Is a cheerful place where neighbours meet together,
With oaken beams and shining red-tiled floor,
Cool in summer, snug in winter weather.

Behind the bar, stands handsome Harry Hare,
Serving nut-brown acorn ale and nips
Of cowslip cordial you won't find elsewhere,
And wine, home-made from rosy hedgerow hips.

While nimble Mrs Hare, his gentle wife,
Serves drinks and tasty food with willing grace,
Seems to enjoy her active busy life,
And welcomes everyone with smiling face.

She it is who has the business brain,
But being a little creature of some tact
And anxious not to cause her husband pain,
Has always managed to conceal this fact.

For no one thought that Harry Hare was clever,
Nor yet that he was absolutely dense;
At least he had no enemies whatever,
And all he really lacked was commonsense.

But neither his wife nor customers knew that
Though he was smart and always cut a dash,
In bold check suit and jaunty bowler hat,
He'd had bad luck and owed a lot of cash.

Athlete and first-rate runner in his day,
He'd got in with a sporty racing set
Of wealthy weasels, who'd led him astray;
Till he was up to his long ears in debt.

Furthermore, he'd talked big, boasted loud,
About 'My job, my inn and my success.'
And spent his hard-earned money on a crowd
Of flashy spivs he wanted to impress . . .

His troubles seemed too great for him to bear,
He brooded over many madcap schemes,
Told not a soul, not even Mrs Hare,
Fretted all day, by night had dreadful dreams.

One day, when doing his accounts alone,
A weasel from the race-course sidled in;
'Hi, Hare, so here's the pub you own,
In good repair both outside and within.

I thought I'd look it over. I'm surprised,
Rememb'ring all you said about the place,
It's so old-fashioned and not modernised.
Needs poshing-up,' he snapped with a grimace.

Harry sat there silent and dismayed,
Convinced the weasel was a debt collector,
Or, which made him even more afraid,
A private eye or a police-inspector.

Weasel, observing he was dumb with fright,
And knowing his financial situation,
Decided that the time was ripe and right
To give the hare a fuller explanation.

'See here,' he said, 'I've money to invest,
And would prefer to place it out of town;
And, hoping it would pay good interest,
I might agree to put a payment down.'

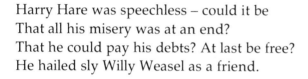

Harry Hare was speechless – could it be
That all his misery was at an end?
That he could pay his debts? At last be free?
He hailed sly Willy Weasel as a friend.

Just then his wife came in with home-made pies,
Freshly baked and smelling quite delicious,
Set them down and, though all ears and eyes,
Said not a word, though feeling most suspicious

Because the weasel looked to her a crook.
She hurried off as it was baking-day,
And, with another batch of pies to cook,
Unluckily, she had no time to stay.

The weasel gave the thankful hare some money,
And handed him a document to sign;
Hare should have thought his business methods funny,
But, keen on cash, signed on the dotted line.

Many harebrained things he'd done before,
But nothing quite so daft and downright silly
As to involve himself and *Friendly Paw*
With anyone as sharp as wily Willy.

When Willy left, well-satisfied,
Harry told his wife what he'd arranged
And was aghast when she sat down and cried,
'What have you done, you must have been deranged!'

He hung his head and told her of his debt,
And how the ready cash would put him straight.
To which she answered, 'How could you forget
We've savings we can use if desperate?

We must at once pay all that money back,
And get the document returned: that's fair,
And you – you must give up the racing-track,
We simply can't afford it, Harry Hare!'

Off to the bank went Mrs Hare next day.
She drew some money from their joint account
And came back happy, for she'd found that they
Could pay the weasel back the whole amount.

Next, they determined, Willy must be found
And told they were withdrawing from the deal;
They had no trouble running him to ground,
For later on he came in for a meal.

After the bar was closed and he replete,
He told them with a condescending air,
He'd much enjoyed the food he'd had to eat,
But for their wine and ale he did not care.

'Something stronger's needed here,' he said.
'Something with more stingo, zip and wow.
Instead of cooking pies and baking bread,
Your lady-wife should grace the bar – and how!

I own a big concern – a factory –
Turns out pies and bread and all that stuff.
And when we get the posh crowd here – you'll see,
Drink's what matters – cheap food's good enough.

We'll get a thick pile carpet on the floor,
Block up the hearth, install a flicker-fire,
TV, Muzak – and a smart decor.
You just won't know the place, I promise, 'Squire.'

So he ran on, till Mrs Hare cried, 'Stop!
Your schemes are fine but here would be no good.
So take your cash – we'll let the matter drop,
And part on friendly terms, that's understood.'

But Willy waved the paper Hare had signed,
And asked her sharply, 'What do you think *this* is?
Read it carefully, *if* you'll be so kind,
I'd like *your* opinion, brainy missis.'

The paper took the form of a receipt:
'Money advanced by Weasel for a share
(which further payments later will complete)
In *Friendly Paw*.' Signed clearly, 'Harry Hare.'

'Good as a contract, eh?' said Weasel, 'Don't
You panic now; we'll soon get organised,
Ever so rich you'll be, see if you won't.
"Pub of the Year", I shouldn't be surprised.'

When he'd gone, they shared a sad dismay,
But clever Mrs Hare was thoughtful, too.
'Though things look bad, perhaps we'll find a way;
We ought to get a legal point of view.'

They went to seek advice which they required,
At Otterholt, the riverbank estate,
Of old John Otter, who was now retired
Though long ago he'd been an advocate.

Seated in his rather chilly room
They laid their case before him quite concisely,
While he listened, mumbling 'ah and h'm,
Oh dear me – and, what do you mean precisely?'

At length, said he, 'The weasel has a case.
Money has changed hands – you've undertaken
To let him have an interest in your place,
And, in law, alas, that can't be shaken.

Unless – unless' – and he held up a paw,
'You prove your customers don't *want* things changed;
That is an avenue you might explore
And a successful outcome be arranged.'

They offered payment, which he waved away,
'I like the *Paw*, the fish you serve is fine;
From now on I shall lunch there every day
And in the evening bring my friends to dine.'

The word went round the village in a flash
That everyone who cared about the fate
Of *Friendly Paw*, must join and help to smash
A bid to alter it before too late.

So the Hares wrote out a grand petition
And got the names of everyone combined;
Even the Mole, though in a frail condition,
Tottered in with Tom and duly signed.

As always is the case, when creatures fight
And sink their diff'rences in common cause
For what they love and what they think is right,
They are the happier for joining paws.

So when the weasel called next time, he heard
A hum of cheerful voices, and the scent
Of homely food, well-cooked and nicely served,
In an atmosphere of comfort and content.

In the ample hearth, a log-fire brightly burned,
Otter presided at a grand fish dinner;
For all of them were anxious and concerned
Hare and not Weasel should end up the winner.

Though Weasel read reproach in all their eyes,
He swaggered to a table and sat down
Close to the fire, and what was his surprise
When Mrs Hare came up without a frown

And served him a hot dinner of the best.
He drank a pint of ale then ordered more,
Stretched himself the better to digest,
Closed his eyes and soon began to snore;

When he woke, he was handed by the otter,
The grand petition, with a formal bow;
For though he thought the weasel was a rotter,
He preferred to act with style – not have a row.

Weasel accepted it but felt quite bad;
For though so used to getting his own way,
To see so many creatures looking sad,
Made him *almost* feel ashamed that day.

However he took his briefcase and departed;
And next morning in his dingy den,
Feeling unaccountably down-hearted,
He looked for Hare's receipt to read again.

He could not find it so he searched his mind,
Finally concluding it had been
At *Friendly Paw* that he'd left it behind,
As he remembered clearly he had seen

It in his case before he started dozing.
Someone might have taken it, but who?
Not much use just wasting time supposing,
He must resolve what it was best to do;

So lying down upon his unmade bed,
He pondered long until he had decided
As without the document the deal was dead,
He'd let them off and say he'd been misguided.

No one – or only one – would know the fact
That he no longer had what Hare had signed;
He'd get the credit for a kindly act,
And folk he'd grown to like, would think him kind.

Almost believing that this last was true,
He hastened to the inn and told them all
That any claim he had he now withdrew.
Their grateful cheers made him feel rather small.

'Drinks on the house!' called thankful Harry Hare,
And Weasel drank, but, looking round the while,
Saw Badger raise his glass with knowing air,
And glance at his parents with a meaning smile:

Willy wondered, but he'd never know,
As loyal Waybeyond would never say
That Badger, nicknamed 'Artful' long ago,
Just *might* have whisked that document away!

Well Done, Rosie Rabbit!

When Rosie Rabbit's husband disappeared,
The gossips winked and foul play was not feared.
'T'was not the fox as carried him away,
But one of them smart bunny-girls they say,
And if Rosie wants him back, she's plain deluded,
Good riddance to bad rabbit,' they concluded.

Meanwhile poor Rosie left – not on her own,
For no one with six children's much alone,
Continued every day to clean and cook,
Yet always opened their one story-book,
When day was done, and round her shabby chair,
Gathered the children that they all might share
After they'd finished supper at the table,
A magic hour of fairy-tale and fable.
But often – as children will – they asked for more,
Until the book slipped from her tired paw.
And once, eyes closed, she found she had invented
A tale herself with which they were contented.

Next day, the rent-man called and much was owing,
As Rosie's husband, being easy-going,
Had cruelly helped himself before he went
From the broken teapot where she kept the rent.

Her youngest tore new trousers on the stairs,
The bill came in for all their shoe repairs;
Without a fire, the house was cold and bleak,
When tiles fell off, the roof began to leak;
There were payments on hire-purchase to maintain,
And lettuce and carrots both went up again.
So late one night while all the children slept,
In her clean but chilly kitchen, Rosie wept.

Later she bravely dried her streaming eyes,
Fetched her account-book, and with many sighs
Listed the calls upon her little purse,
Though, seen in black-and-white, they seemed far worse.
In fact the figures gave her such a fright,
She turned the page to hide them out of sight,
Stared at the blank lined paper, seized her pen,
And all night did not lay it down again,
Except to brew refreshing parsley tea,
And look-up spelling in her dictionary.
For since her children liked the tales she told,
It had struck her that such stories might be *sold*!

So for many a night with zeal to be admired,
She wrote and feeling hopeful was not tired,
And though the cost of postage was a ramp,
She forewent parsley tea to buy a stamp,
Sent off her stories on an April day,
And heard no more until the end of May.
And, by then feeling downcast and dejected,
She heard one morning – they had been *accepted*!
It was at breakfast Rosie got the letter,
Almost spoke, then thought that it was better
To tell her splendid news when school was done.

So saw them off and hugged them everyone.

But the instant they were gone, she made a list
Of delicious things to eat they'd often missed,
Then hurried out and, in the village store,
Enjoyed her shopping and not feeling poor.
As well as food, she bought some games and toys,
Wool to knit jackets for her girls and boys,
Blouses and shirts and 'with-it' boiler-suits,
Caps and scarves and zip-up cowboy boots,
A table-cloth and pretty dinner set.
And – most important – she did not forget
Her new career; so, lastly, also took
Pens, foolscap paper and a big notebook.

Later, the children hurried home from school,
Expecting a frugal meal, for as a rule
Though Rosie did her best, she was not able
To put all she would like upon the table;
But nearing home today, they sniffed with glee
The smell of fresh baked carrot cake for tea.
They hastened in and there before their eyes
Was spread their mother's wonderful surprise:
New china and a lacey cloth were laid
With tasty sandwiches and cakes home-made,
And at each place for every happy child,
Tinsel-wrapped, well-chosen gifts were piled.

Oh what a scene of joy and satisfaction,
Rosie was bunny-hugged quite to distraction,
And when at story-time, she read aloud
One of her tales, and saw how very proud
Her children were, it was all that she could do
Not to shed happy tears but read it through.

And when they clapped their paws and cried, 'Please,
                                          Mother,'
She let them stay up late and read another...
Publication of her book was not delayed,
It was out in time to catch the Christmas trade.
And at New Year, the publishers wrote to tell her
Sales were so good – she'd written a best-seller!

To Waybeyond came carloads of the Press,
To feature 'Rabbit Writer's Great Success'.
'Mother of Six Exclusively reveals,
My Rags to Riches Story – How it Feels'.
A photo of Rosie, 'Seated at Her Desk'.
(The kitchen table) looking picturesque,
Pen in paw, brow creased with concentration:
'Famous Author Seeks for Inspiration'.
Unspoiled by all this foolish ballyhoo,
Rosie continued as she used to do,
Putting her children first, but now carefree
From money worries, debt and misery.

'Now that our Rosie's rich,' the gossips said,
With many a knowing look and nodding head,
'T'is clear her rascal husband – let's be frank,
Has never heard she's money in the bank,
Or he'd be back before you say Jack Rabbit,
To spend it on himself as was his habit.
T'was really the best action of his life,
When he deserted children, home and wife,
For if she'd not been left in sorry plight,
Perhaps she'd not have found out she could write,
And with her pen keep want and care away.
Well done, Rosie Rabbit, 's what we say!'

The Night-Watchman

Cyril Squirrel, dapper, debonair,
Bustles to the bank at five to nine,
Spruce and freshly-brushed and groomed with care,
With a rolled umbrella even when it's fine.
And, as the clock chimes from the nearby tower,
He unlocks the door – precisely on the hour,
Then looks into his tidy office,where
Woodwork gleams and polished brasses shine.

Before his staff arrives – it numbers two,
He inspects the safe and has a sharp look round,
A task he never fails to carry through
To see that all's in order, safe and sound,
For ever since the unsuccessful raid
Upon the post-office, he's been afraid –
In spite of burglar-bolts and bells – all new –
He wants a watchman but one can't be found.

Last week from his head-office he'd received
A letter that was terse and somewhat tough:
'Re. night-watchman, what has been achieved,
And are you confident you've done enough?'
'Enough!' he'd snapped at all his staff in rage,
He'd not seen anyone he could engage;
His pride was hurt, his feelings most aggrieved,
He smarted from the undeserved rebuff.

They should know how hard it was these days
For a post of trust to find somebody right.
He'd advertised in many different ways,
But no one wanted to sit up all night.
At last, one winter's day, he got a letter,
Which cheered him up and made him feel much better.
Though badly spelt (he feared his hopes to raise).
It was, at least, well-written and polite:

'Dear Sir,' it said, 'I takes the libety
Of applying for the job you advertize,
I'm young and keen and if you will take me,
I'll garentee to never close me eyes.
I'm small but you will find me strong and brave.
Dormouse is me name, but call me Dave.
P.S I will call round so you can see
Wether you likes me or contrarywise.'

When Cyril saw the tiny candidate
In woolly cap and jeans and sweater dressed,
Neat and punctual – not a second late,
He wondered if perhaps it might be best
Not to admit he'd found no one at all,
But try the dormouse – though he *was* so small;

He looked a decent chap at any rate,
Quiet, respectful, very self-possessed.

He gathered that he had a widowed mother,
Who took in washing and was known to be
A decent soul, and also had a brother
Who'd left the village, whom he did not see
Except on holidays, when he returned
To bring his mother money he had earned.
It seemed they were all good to one another
And were an honest happy family.

So he offered Dave the job, and saw
A beaming smile light up his little face.
And to head-office wrote therefore
To tell them he had filled the watchman's place . . .
Next evening when the staff had gone at five,
He waited for the dormouse to arrive.
Who, sharp on time, came laden through the door
With a rug, a thermos-flask and heavy case.

'Here I am – good-evening, sir,' he cried,
'Mother's loaded me with all this gear,
No chance to leave without it, though I tried,
Telling her she'd wreck my new career!'
Cyril led the eager young recruit
Around the bank and hoped that he would suit,
Then settled him with chair and torch inside,
Having made th'alarm-bell system clear.

At nine o'clock next day and every day,
He found the watchman wide-awake and bright.
Cyril began to think him worth his pay

And slept himself more peacefully at night;
Until head-office wrote to him again:
'*A dormouse watchman* – you must be insane.
They are not only weak and small, but they
Are always dozing – he must go outright!'

Cyril *was* distressed – he'd been so keen
To do the best he could, he hadn't thought
Of this – how crassly stupid he had been.
Dormice were by nature drowsy. Overwrought
Till dawn, he tossed and turned then out he crept
Back to the bank to see if dormouse slept,
Trusting to luck that he would not be seen;
So undignified – if he were caught!

The village was all dark except a glow
Showing from one window in the lane
And as it shone from Dormouse Bungalow,
He stopped to look in through the window-pane;
And what he saw caused him such pained surprise,
He scarcely could believe his own two eyes:
For there was Dormouse, moving to-and-fro,
Turning his mother's mangle, plain as plain.

The bank left unattended! Cyril sped
On to the bank and, with a trembling paw,
Agitated, full of fear and dread,
Turned the key and opened wide the door.
But in that instant, quickly as a flash,
A smartly wielded truncheon hit him – bash!
He staggered back holding his aching head,
Tripped and fell upon the polished floor.

And to his great amazement as he fell,
Instead of helping him upon his feet,
The doughty dormouse pressed the burglar-bell,
And tied him up with knots both tight and neat,
Indifferent to his mounting indignation
At such an idiotic situation,
As being treated like a criminal.
His rage and stupefaction were complete.

He closed his eyes, t'was all too much for him
And when again he opened them, he saw
A sight that made his reeling senses swim:
Two dormice where there'd been but *one* before!
Shock had made his mind give way no doubt,
He felt too weak to think the matter out . . .
His bonds were loosed, he ached in every limb,
Then someone helped him up with gentle paw.

A dormouse brought him water, all the same
He blinked, and saw, or thought he saw, another.
Till one said, 'Des or Desmond is my name
And Dave, your employee, is my *twin*-brother.
I'm out of work – he feared to fall asleep,
So turn-about, watch on the bank we keep.
He knows you – I do not, so when you came
I biffed you one while Dave was helping mother.'

Just then appeared the constable, Sam Stoat,
Who produced his pencil and his book.
'Alarm went off at six,' he made a note,
'I proceeded to the bank to find the crook.'
But he only saw poor Cyril, who was bruised,
And two small dormice, frightened and confused.

Then Cyril who'd been thinking, cleared his throat,
And turning to the twins, their paws he shook.

'These two brave lads,' he said, 'who guard the bank,
Will never let a thief in I'll be bound;
I was not sure of them – I will be frank –
And to see if they were wide-awake, came round.
No sooner did they hear me turn my key
Than, with a bound, they fell on top of me,
And my head-office will have me to thank
For having such efficient watchmen found.

Stoat was disappointed, he had hoped
At last to lock a villain in his jail
And be commended for the way he'd coped,
And tell at *Friendly Paw*, the thrilling tale;
He sighed, saluted Cyril, went his way . . .
Dave and Des did not know what to say,
And Cyril's injured head made him feel doped,
But he'd a scheme he trusted would not fail.

The truth was that he very much preferred
The night's proceedings to remain unknown
Except in Waybeyond where they occurred.
To write or narrate on the telephone
So strange a drama to the powers-that-be,
Involving him in loss of dignity
Would harm his image, make him look absurd.
So to the twins he said in kindly tone:

'I believe you're unemployed.' He turned to Des,
'And I've been thinking that we might agree
A plan I've made if you and Dave say yes,

To suit your mother, both of you and me:
In my bachelor pad, that's neat and small,
For sometime past I've had no one at all
To garden, help with chores; and I confess
From all these tasks I gladly would be free.

What d'you say to working turn-about,
Taking alternate nights to guard the bank,
Alternate days to work where I hang-out?
It would suit me well – I will be frank.'
The twins both smiled at him and one another,
It would suit them too and please their mother;
They'd feared that giving Cyril such a clout
Might have made their future prospects blank.

'Another thing,' said Cyril, 'I propose
To give a kind of bonus every year
If neither of you drop asleep or doze,
To Mrs Dormouse, whom you both hold dear.'
He knew this was a crafty manoeuvre,
Their mother being a forceful character,
Known for being a tartar when she chose,
Who, if the twins were slack, would be severe.

Head-office when they heard the news from Cyril –
That single-pawed a dormouse had succeeded
In knocking-down and tying-up a squirrel –
Felt they had the watchman that they needed.
Which, as he was most careful not to state
He was the squirrel, was quite accurate!

THE END